Text and illustrations copyright © 2007 by Nick Bruel
A Neal Porter Book
Published by Roaring Brook Press

New edition ISBN: 978-1-59643-844-6

Roaring Brook Press is a division of Holtzbrinck Publishing Holdings Limited Partnership, 175 Fifth Avenue, New York, New York 10010

The Library of Congress has cataloged the earlier edition as follows:
Bruel, Nick.
Poor Puppy / by Nick Bruel. —
1st ed.   p. cm.
"A Neal Porter book."

Summary: When Bad Kitty won't play with him, Poor Puppy has to amuse himself with an alphabetical list of toys and dreams of playing in an alphabetical list of countries.

GROCERY LIST--
- MILK
- EGGS
CAT FOOD!

FOR JOHN, JOHANNA + MIKAELA

ISBN: 978-1-59643-270-3
[1. Alphabet—Fiction.
2. Dogs—Fiction.
3. Cats—Fiction.]
I. Title.

PZ7.B82832Poo 2007
[E]—dc22
2006032191

mackids.com

Roaring Brook Press books are available for special promotions and premiums. For details contact: Director of Special Markets, Holtzbrinck Publishers

First edition 2007 New edition 2012
Printed in China by South China Printing Co. Ltd., Dongguan City, Guangdong Province
10 9 8 7 6 5 4 3 2 1

Puppy's
best
friend
is
Kitty.

But Puppy
is sad.

**Kitty doesn't
want to play
with him
today.**

Poor Puppy.

Poor, poor Puppy.

Poor, poor, poor, poor,

POOR

Puppy!

**Instead of Kitty,
the only things
Puppy has to play
with are . . .**

1 AIRPLANE

2 BALLS

3 CARS

4 Dolls

5 Electric Trains

6 Finger Puppets

7 GLOWSTICKS

8 HULA HOOPS

11 Kites

12 Liters of Fingerpaints

13 Marbles

14 Nutcrackers

15 Old cat toys he found under the sofa

16 Pinwheels

17 Queens, Kings, Knights, Bishops, Castles and Pawns

18 Robots

19 Soccer Balls

20 Teddy Bears

21 **U**KULELES

22 **V**ALENTINES

23 WIND-UP TOYS

24 BOXES OF CRAYONS

25 **Y**o-Yos

AND 26 **Z**oo ANIMALS

That was FUN!
But Puppy really wanted to
play with Kitty.

Poor Puppy.

Now he's so tired,
he has to take a nap.

Poor Puppy.

**When Puppy naps,
he dreams.**

**What do you think
he dreams about?**

He dreams about playing with Kitty, of course!

They play . . .

. . . Puppy wakes up.

What a great dream!
Now Puppy is so happy,
he wants to play!

And so does Kitty!

HOORAY!